Uglješa Šajtinac
Huddersfield

English version by Chris Thorpe

from a translation by Duška Radosavljević

OBERON BOOKS

LONDON

First published in 2004 by Oberon Books Ltd.
521 Caledonian Road, London N7 9RH
Tel: +44 (0) 20 7607 3637 / Fax: +44 (0) 20 7607 3629
e-mail: info@oberonbooks.com
www.oberonbooks.com

A catalogue record for this book is available from the British Library.

PB ISBN: 9781840024494

Armley Photo by West Yorkshire Archive Service, Leeds.

Visit www.oberonbooks.com to read more about all our books and to buy them. You will also find features, author interviews and news of any author events, and you can sign up for e-newsletters so that you're always first to hear about our new releases.

Introduction

If you were to choose one truly European playwright who had an international career in his lifetime – the likelihood is that he lived at the turn of the twentieth century. He also lived or travelled abroad and enjoyed a wide circle of acquaintances who championed his universally appealing work in their respective countries.

Several decades down the line and – Europe stands divided. The playwrights who made it across the Curtain were usually political dissidents – championed only by halves. Worse still, a country like the Socialist Yugoslavia – the most 'liberal' exponent of the monolithic East, with its movies and rock'n'roll – had no dissidence to boast of. With the budding talent of the 1960s, Yugoslavian theatre did become a surrogate forum and even a political hotspot. But Tito preferred cinematic entertainment. He subsidised theatre and the international exchange, such as the world-famous Bitef Festival, and left it all to self-censorship. Interestingly however, Yugoslav drama concerned itself with idiosyncratic issues: the details of local history when it was serious, and the nuances of (multi)-national character for comic value. This navel-gazing naturally continued when, following 1989, the country started cannibalising itself, plunging into further isolation and letting its young disperse all over the world.

Still, Yugoslavian canon did contribute several noteworthy plays to the European stage – from the sisteenth century comedies by Croatia's Marin Držić and the modern classics by Branislav Nušic´ and Miroslav Krleža, to the challenging contemporary tragedies by Biljana Srbljanović. The region's most notable living playwright Dušan Kovačević also has a string of international awards for his work including the Palme d'Or winning *Underground.*

Recently re-invented democratic Serbia is inevitably generating new issues for consideration. Co-incidentally, its theatre has a charming and accomplished young playwright with a love of travel and socialising – Uglješa Šajtinac.

Although steeped in tradition, Uglješa's plays are blessed with a special talent for turning the specific into the universal. Following the Huddersfield premiere of his moving debut about the 'generation gap' – *The Propsmaster* – in 2000, he brings you *Huddersfield,* a play about 'turning thirty'. A world premiere of *Huddersfield,* in Chris Thorpe's brilliant culture-sensitive version, is also the very first British production of a Serbian play. Or should I say – a new 'truly European play'?

Duška Radosavljević

Characters

FATHER
sixty

RASHA
thirty

IVAN
thirty

MILLIE
sixteen

DOOLE
thirty

IGOR
thirty

Time: 24 hours

Place: the lounge

Setting: Zrenjarin, northern Serbia

First performance at the Courtyard Theatre, West Yorkshire Playhouse, Saturday 15 May 2004, with the following company:

Dylan Brown	IVAN
Claire Lams	MILLIE
John Lightbody	RASHA
Nick Moss	DOOLE
Robert Pickavance	FATHER
Toby Sawyer	IGOR

Director	Alex Chisholm
Designer	Emma Williams
Lighting Designer	Tim Skelly
Sound Designer	Mic Pool
Fight Director	Renny Krupinski
Dialect Coach	Mark Langley
Casting	Kay Magson
Assistant Stage Manager	Christine Guthrie

I Fucked Your Mother

The lounge. RASHA sits at the table, smoking and sipping coffee. In the background we hear noise and mumbling. FATHER's voice.

FATHER: *I FUCKED YOUR MOTHER, you FUCKING MOTHERFUCKER!*

RASHA sits calmly, sipping coffee.

FATHER rushes in. He is ferociously angry and blind drunk.

Are you deaf?

…

You cloth-eared cunt? Eh?

…

Taken the piss for thirty fucking years!

RASHA: Morning, Dad. Coffee?

FATHER: Coffee!? Let's see. Will I have some coffee *in my own front room*!? You cheeky little bastard! That's *my* fucking coffee you're offering me! Every-fucking-thing in here is mine! What have *you* ever contributed? Eh? *Eh?*

RASHA: Nothing.

FATHER: I beg your fucking pardon?

RASHA: I said, nothing.

FATHER: That's it. You can get to fuck… When I get back, you're gone, understand!? Go on, just leave… I don't give a flying fuck where to…! Car keys!

FATHER holds his hand out.

RASHA gets up, passes the keys to him.

FATHER: Right! I'm gonna sell the bastard! Fuck it! It's my fucking car, isn't it? What's it to you!?

RASHA: Nothing.

FATHER: What?

RASHA: Nothing.

FATHER: Nothing! That's you all over, son!

RASHA gets up and heads for the toilet.

Where the fuck are you going?

RASHA: For a shit.

FATHER: Like fuck you are! Not on *my* bog! Go and shit in the street!

FATHER goes to the toilet door and pulls it off its hinges. He holds it stubbornly in the air.

What? Hey, is it my door? Yes it fucking is! So I can do what I bloody well like with it...

FATHER goes to the front door.

RASHA watches him.

RASHA: You've taken the door.

FATHER: So I have! What's it to you? Get your bags packed and fuck off! You don't live here anymore! Is that clear? I don't give a shot where you end up. Move to England, eh? Fuck off to Canada! Go and find the rest of the fuckers who let this country down! You fucking motherfucker...!

FATHER goes out with the door in his hands.

RASHA goes to the toilet and sits. Looks into the room. Looks at the toilet door frame.

Knocking at the front door.

RASHA: Christ... Yes!

IVAN enters, carrying a small book. Looks around. Shuts the door behind him.

IVAN: Rasha?

RASHA: Make yourself at home. I'm having a shit.

IVAN comes to the table, sits down.

RASHA gets up from the toilet, comes out.

I can't.

IVAN: Well there was shouting, so I assumed you were awake... I brought you 'The Tale of Spiritual Life' by Father Neil Sorski. Remember? I promised to bring it round.

RASHA: Yeah. Coffee?

IVAN: Okay. You know? The book I was telling you about? The one about the eight sinful thoughts.

RASHA: Eight. As many as that?

IVAN: Eight. Succumbing to fleshly appetites, lust, greed for material goods, anger, sorrow, melancholy, vanity and pride.

RASHA: He took the door away. The last defence against indignity. Can't even have a shit.

IVAN: You and your father had a fight?

RASHA: We don't fight in this house. We just try to put up with each other.

IVAN: Why did they let him leave when he's still drinking?

RASHA: He's beyond help.

IVAN: He has to stop. Make sure he reads the book too. He's got to pray and beseech the Lord to help him. And

he mustn't forget that Judgement Day's approaching...
Now, those are just the first two steps. In fact, there are
four steps altogether –

RASHA: Okay, leave it for now. I'll read it... I will.

IVAN: Human sin's a gradual process, you see. Firstly,
we have SUGGESTION – when demonic whispers
penetrate your thoughts or your imagination. It's
confronted even the greatest minds. The second level?
CONSENT. During CONSENT you wrestle with your
sinful thoughts, leading to CONFINEMENT, the third
level. At this point a *supreme* effort's needed to banish
evil thoughts – even with God's help. And then...then
the most terrible...the fourth level...

Knocking at the front door.

RASHA: Come in!

MILLIE enters.

Come in...he even took the key...

MILLIE: Hi. You forgotten?

RASHA: Course not. Ivan, this is Millie, my student.

IVAN: Ivan. Pleased to meet you.

RASHA: Ivan's cool. Come and join the service. We've just
got to the fourth level...

MILLIE: Of what?

RASHA: Sin.

IVAN: Yes. That's PASSION. Enduring pleasure,
transformed into habit. Slavery to sin. The...the
pornography of the soul. It requires immense willpower
and a struggle of titanic proportions to return to the
right path.

...

Excuse me.

IVAN gets up and starts to go.

RASHA: You haven't drunk your coffee.

IVAN: I told mother I wouldn't be long. Rasha, sorry, could I...if I could bring you – another poem? You wouldn't have to read it there and then... Could I do that?

RASHA: Oh... Okay, yeah.

IVAN goes. Shuts the door behind him.

MILLIE throws herself at RASHA, kisses him on the mouth – a long, passionate kiss. She puts his hand between her legs.

Jesus you're so wet...

MILLIE: Sure am...

RASHA: Ready for this, then?

RASHA undoes his trousers.

MILLIE smiles and moves away from him.

MILLIE: So, who's the freak?

...

Hey?

MILLIE looks down. She sees IVAN's book on the table.

What's the book?

MILLIE picks up the book and leafs through it.

(*Reads.*) 'Keep yourself away from women, from conversing with them and looking at them; also avoid living with young, feminine and pretty faces and refrain from looking at them...' What's this crap?

RASHA: Leave it...

RASHA goes to stroke her face but she moves away, looking around.

MILLIE: This place is a fucking pigsty! So...shag first, or Hamlet?

...

I've got an exam on Monday –

RASHA: Yeah, well *I'm* dying for a shit –

MILLIE: Then have one.

RASHA: I can't. My fucking father took the toilet door off.

Knocking at the front door.

Alright, Ivan! Come in!

MILLIE: Jesus...

MILLIE goes over to examine the toilet.

IVAN enters with a sheet of paper in his hand.

IVAN: That's it. It's called 'The Snail'...

MILLIE: Rasha –

RASHA: *What?*

MILLIE: Surely there's a *place*...you could get your father some help...

RASHA: Oh yeah? A place? What kind of place would that be, Millie?

MILLIE: I dunno. Some kind of...institution?

RASHA: Institution?

MILLIE: Well –

RASHA: Oh! You want to sent my father to a *loony bin.*

...

Ivan. Millie's interested in what it's like being in a loony bin...

MILLIE: I am not.

RASHA: Sounds like you fucking are. Believe me, we're in the presence of an expert. Come on Ivan. What's a typical day in a loony bin like?

IVAN looks uncomfortable.

RASHA takes the poem from him, and begins to skim through it. He gestures encouragingly to IVAN.

IVAN: Can I sit down?

RASHA: Please do.

IVAN: The nurse switches on the dormitory light every morning at quarter to six...

RASHA notices MILLIE's lack of interest.

RASHA: Sorry, mate... Millie, listen and learn.

MILLIE sits down grudgingly. Her interest gradually increases as IVAN goes on.

Carry on, Ivan.

IVAN: The patients jump out of their beds like they were obeying orders. Due to overcrowding, there's a long queue for the toilet. The luckiest guy's obviously the one who gets there first...

MILLIE laughs, so does IVAN.

RASHA: What's funny? At least the mentalists get to shit like normal people, even if they have to queue for it. Was there a door on the bog?

IVAN: Yes.

RASHA: There you go. Even the loony bin's got toilet doors. I'm the only one that hasn't...

IVAN: Shall I go on?

MILLIE: Ivan, I'm... You don't have to...

RASHA: You – shut it. Get a pen and paper! Take some notes! Go on, Ivan.

IVAN: Everything happens really fast in the morning. You have to make your bed, get dressed, get ready for your exercise. Then it's twenty minutes relaxation in this filthy room. It's called the 'smoke-room' so it's coffee and a morning cigarette. Then – breakfast.

RASHA: What's for breakfast?

IVAN: Baby food.

MILLIE: *Really?*

IVAN: Cheese spread. Puréed bananas. Stuff that was easy to chew. Sometimes there'd be an omelette or some ham, but then...the wars... Then, after breakfast, everyone splits up: carpenter's workshop, joiner's workshop, art studio.

RASHA: Where were you?

IVAN: For a few months, I was in the art studio.

RASHA: Painting?

IVAN: No. I sculpted. In wood.

RASHA: Hm? And it went well?

IVAN: Not too well, no. I mean the teacher liked my stuff... but it was mediocre.

RASHA: Will you show us some?

IVAN: If I can find it. It's somewhere in the cellar... Sorry.

I've got to get back. Rasha, please just have a look at the poem, tell me what you think.

IVAN leaves, RASHA glances at the poem.

RASHA: There you are. Moral of the story? Even the loony bin's got toilet doors.

MILLIE: Oh, fuck the doors!

MILLIE takes hold of a curtain, rips it down and hangs it in the toilet doorway.

Well you've got a curtain now. Stylish, eh?

RASHA: Very cool.

MILLIE: Could've done it yourself.

RASHA: I could have. But I'm known for doing nothing. It's my way of paying my debt to society.

MILLIE: Well do something for me and have a fucking shit.

RASHA goes through the curtain into the toilet. He takes IVAN's poem with him.

RASHA: This is better. I'm not used to shitting in front of people. Makes it hard to concentrate… Right … 'The Snail'…!

MILLIE: No way! There's a fucking snail in the bog?

RASHA: No. That's the title of Ivan's poem…! So, 'The Snail'…

(*Reads.*) 'You miraculous creature
with a house on your back
carrying a home on your own spine
You crawl, looking for food
Waiting for the rain
So that you can take a walk on the wet side

Glistening in the grass, bedewed
You slide down the raindrop
Cursed!
All alone!
Your home has enough room
only for yourself and no one else
And you maybe
Spent all your life
Looking for someone
To invite inside
Someone to share
A cup of tea
Or coffee with'
…This is phenomenal!

MILLIE: Jesus. He's really fucking mental.

MILLIE leafs through the book again.

RASHA: He's okay. Not overly insane.

MILLIE: What's he on about then?

RASHA: He's intelligent. Fucked up but high functioning. Got these fantastic powers of recall. It's his mum that's nuts – Ivan's just neurotic.

MILLIE: Oh my God! (*Reading from the same book…*) 'And if at all possible, do not stay with them on your own, says Vasiliy the Great, not even in most exceptional circumstances; for nothing is more important to you than your soul for whose sake Christ has died and risen'…

RASHA: Don't stay with who on your own?

MILLIE: Girls, I should think…

RASHA: The man's got a point.

MILLIE: What a pile of shit.

The toilet flushes.

RASHA re-enters.

RASHA: Took the words right out of my mouth. (*To himself.*) What the fuck's he going to do? Waltzing down the street with a fucking door?

MILLIE: Rasha…make sure you're clean.

RASHA: What do you mean?

MILLIE: Give yourself a wash…your…*bits.*

RASHA: Why?

MILLIE: Because I want us to try…that thing.

RASHA: Do you?

MILLIE: Yeah.

RASHA: You'll kiss it? You'll put it in your mouth?

MILLIE: Yes!

Mongolia

MILLIE and RASHA are lying on a mattress in the lounge. RASHA is smoking and sleepy. MILLIE is restless.

MILLIE: That was… Just…having it in your mouth when it's getting hard. It was great… Wasn't it?

RASHA: Mhm…

MILLIE: Did you let other girls…?

RASHA: Mhm…

MILLIE: Some guy, he was blackmailing Anita, right? Like, 'I'm not gonna fuck you unless you give me a blow job, I just can't get it up 'til it's been in your mouth…'

RASHA: Mhm…

MILLIE: Hey, is your video working?

RASHA: Mhm...

MILLIE: I've got something to show you...

MILLIE goes to the table, takes a videotape from her bag, slots it in.

A man and a woman can be heard having sex.

RASHA watches.

RASHA: What the fuck's this?

MILLIE: Watch.

RASHA: Where did you get this from?

MILLIE: Shut up. Tell me about Hamlet. And I'll be touching myself.

RASHA: You mad bitch...

MILLIE: Hamlet! Hamlet! Hamlet!

RASHA: Want me to tell you about Hamlet...? Fair enough... Fucking hell. Eurasian cheekbones. Really sexy... You're a genuine Mongolian, you know...

MILLIE: I'm not.

RASHA: Oh yes you are... Once upon a time, some big Mongolian invader got the hots for your great-great-granny or whatever, and they made a little Mongolian. That little Mongolian made your grandad's grandad, and it goes on and on and on, until we've got this hot little Mongolian girl steaming about everywhere... No, you should be proud of that... They're a fucking proud race, the Mongols, and they'll rise again, one day... They'll come back and fuck us all up! All except you... 'Cos when they see you, they'll say – ah, here she is! Our little princess! Revenge over us upstart Christians...

At your whim! Our Princess, who shall the horses'
tails rip limb from limb? Whose gullet shall we pour
the molten lead into...? And you, you'll look at them
disdainfully from your silken throne... Ruthless... No
mercy shown to any fucker... And they'll never know
where you got that terrifying, warm expression on your
face... And they'll never find out, either, because the
only one who knows the answer will be gone...

MILLIE: And who's that...?

RASHA: Who do you think?

MILLIE: You...

RASHA: Dead right... Your Highness...

MILLIE: So why won't you be there...? You think I'd let
my Mongolians kill you...? They'd never disobey their
long lost princess...

RASHA: I'll have met my maker long before they get here.
I'm already cursed.

MILLIE: So what's the secret?

RASHA: About the princess?

MILLIE: Yes... Why does her face look so terrifying and...

RASHA: Terrifying and warm...? That's 'cos under her
robes...in that regal warmth between her legs...in her
little wet palace...the princess is hiding her fingers...

MILLIE: Do you love me...?

RASHA: No... But I'll find us a field where the grass is
as high as Genghis Khan's eye. We can fuck there.
Mongolian style. Okay?

MILLIE: Yeah.

...

Okay.

RASHA absent-mindedly stares at the screen.

RASHA: Look at him... Spreading his tart apart... Where do they get these fuckers?

MILLIE: How should I know?

...

D'you feel like a bit more Hamlet?

RASHA: Hamlet. The poor fucker... Screwed up by Poppa Hamlet. And he was a bullshitter. A dateless, shagless wonder. Started on the psychedelics to cheer himself up a bit and even then all he ever saw was his fucking dad's ghost. So all the time he was tripping he had this poisonous hallucination to contend with. Always on his back, calling out for *vengeance.*

MILLIE: Basically a tosser, then?

RASHA: Yes. Paternally twisted as well. Sold his Kingdom to feed his habit in the end. Oedipal little bastard too. Hard on for his Mum and an impotent, traitorous wanker.

MILLIE: Put your finger in me...

The telephone rings.

RASHA: I can do better than that...

The telephone keeps ringing.

RASHA jumps up and answers.

Hello! Yeah it's still... No... Igor...? Iggy...! Where the fuck are you, dickhead...? Here? As in, *here*...? Nah, I'm not busy... Fuck, it's been ten, no... Eleven...! Eleven. Fucking. Years!

RASHA covers the speaker, turns to MILLIE.

Fucking turn that down…!

MILLIE turns the volume down with a remote control.

You're in town, then…! No. Still in the same old place…
Me and the old fella… Just us… I'll fill you in when you
turn up, fucker! With Doole? Yeah – come down, both
of you…! This afternoon… He knows… Great, see you!

Hangs up.

…

Iggy!

…

Well fuck me.

MILLIE: I should get to school…

RASHA: Fuck it off.

MILLIE: Oh yeah?

RASHA: Why the fuck should you bother? We can do
some more on Hamlet… And Igor's coming round!
We've not seen each other for eleven years.

MILLIE: Why?

RASHA: He's been away. Living in England.

MILLIE: Great.

RASHA: I'll have to get some beers in…

MILLIE: Fuck beer. Let's have wine. Red wine.

RASHA: Fuck wine! You can drink beer like the rest of us.

MILLIE: Fuck you, then! I'll go out and get my own.

RASHA: Do what you want.

MILLIE: Is there any weed?

RASHA: I'll sort it out.

MILLIE: Nice one.

   …

   And… Hamlet?

RASHA: Hamlet fell by the wayside. Tempted. Lost it. Bad tripped himself into tragedy. Not a funny guy. Dark side. Guys like him should be eliminated.

   …

MILLIE: Fuck me.

RASHA: Don't worry. For fuck's sake who are these two? They've been at it like this for half an hour –

MILLIE: You wanna know? Given you the horn, has it?

RASHA: This shit? No way…

MILLIE: Liar.

   …

   If you only knew.

RASHA: Who the fuck are they then?

MILLIE: Mum and dad.

RASHA: Mum –

MILLIE: Rasha… Meet my parents.

RASHA: You little slut.

MILLIE: Says you? Bitch?

   MILLIE pulls RASHA on top of her.

   They fall onto the mattress.

In the Meantime

MILLIE is on the phone, behind the curtain, in the toilet.

MILLIE: I know you're in school, Anita, fuck off... Yeah, well I had things to do, like I said... Yes, *that*, and it was fucking brilliant... Melts in your mouth (*Laughs*.) ... How the fuck would I know? Never did it to...to someone I didn't love... Listen, fuck the last period off. Meet me in an hour and I'll talk you through it, start to finish... Yeah... Hey, did you get paid...? Cool. Can you bring that cash with you too? Need to get some stuff for later.

Knocking at the door.

Fuck. That's the door... I'm in the toilet! See you in an hour –

Knocking again, then IVAN comes in.

IVAN: Rasha...?

MILLIE: Yeah, there. I've got to go...

MILLIE puts her head through the curtain, her shoulders and arms are bare.

Rasha's out.

IVAN: I really need to speak to him.

MILLIE: He's out...

IVAN: When? I didn't hear him go...

MILLIE: I can't talk to you in this state, Ivan.

IVAN: Did he say when he'll be back?

MILLIE: No.

IVAN ignores her and sits at the table.

IVAN: I'll wait. He has to help me. I'm on the horns of a dilemma. A decision.

MILLIE: Do me a favour, then?

IVAN: Yes.

MILLIE: Leave the room for a minute while I get dressed…

IVAN: All right.

IVAN leaves.

MILLIE comes out wrapped up in a towel, takes her clothes, looks towards the front door and goes back behind the curtain.

MILLIE: You can come in!

IVAN comes in, looks around slowly and goes back to sit at the table.

IVAN: That was quick!

…

Where are you?

MILLIE: Getting dressed in here!

IVAN: Oh! You don't need to worry.

…

I wouldn't try to look at you…

MILLIE: You wouldn't? Great!

MILLIE comes out in her underwear.

Ivan looks around, then looks away, confused.

I can finish up in here, then, can't I…?

MILLIE continues to get dressed.

Course you wouldn't look at me... I bet you wouldn't shag me, either...

IVAN gets up angrily, looks at MILLIE, turns away and goes towards the door.

MILLIE goes after him and stops him.

IVAN turns back, confused and angry.

Ivan... Sorry.

...

Look, I got pissed off 'cos you just walked in here... If you'd waited I'd've let you in...

...

You've got to respect –

IVAN: I thought Rasha was in. It was my mistake. I just – ...

MILLIE: You sit here and wait for Rasha. I've got to be somewhere, there's no one at home, and I don't have a key.

MILLIE goes to the toilet to finish dressing, IVAN returns slowly to the table and sits in 'his' place.

IVAN: Can you forgive me? It was my fault. I made an honest mistake.

...

MILLIE: So what kind of an important decision is it...? I mean if it's not some kind of secret?

She comes back out, grooming herself.

IVAN: Far from it. I write, you know. Stories...poems...and Rasha encouraged me once, and so I carried on. Every day. Two or three lines a day, some times as much as a complete sentence. Hardly ever more. Every day, though. Rasha's an excellent writer. He gave me some of his stories to read –

MILLIE: Seriously?

IVAN: Of course. He's never shown you any? They're a bit...dark. Very good, nonetheless. Wrote poems for a while too. I never read those. Rasha said they weren't any good... And that's how I feel about...everything I've done so far. I've just re-read it. All of it. And it's awful. I'm considering...

MILLIE: What?

...

What were you –

IVAN: Burning the lot of it.

MILLIE: Really?

IVAN: Yes. I read it...and I can only see...weaknesses. The sentences don't...they don't even seem to be mine...a total absence of progress...

MILLIE: Fantastic! Stick around and wait for Rasha, Ivan. I have to go. Say I'll be back soon when you see him...

IVAN: What's keeping him?

MILLIE: He's gone to sort some weed out for later.

...

Should have a smoke yourself, Ivan.

...

It might calm you down.

MILLIE goes out.

IVAN: I can't. Not in my state...

IVAN gets up. Turns, looks around the room. Looks down. Sees something on the floor beside the mattress. He goes over and carefully picks the object up. It's a pair of lace knickers. IVAN is perplexed.

At the same moment FATHER enters, hungover, irritable.

IVAN is frozen with the knickers in his hand.

Oblivious, FATHER puts a carrier bag on the table. From the bag he slowly removes a bottle of brandy, a piece of ham and a piece of cheese.

Good afternoon.

FATHER: Oh…! Afternoon young man… You quite alright…? Not as if you'd know, I suppose… Hungry? Thirsty? Both…? Jesus… You look like you've shat yourself!

IVAN: I'm waiting.

…

For Rasha.

FATHER: On guard duty, are we?

IVAN: There was a girl here –

FATHER: Aha! Knickers! You and my son got shagged, then did you…? Hey, no problem…good thing, a healthy shagging! If you'd started earlier, you might've both grown up by now…

FATHER exits, re-enters with a knife, sits down and starts eating. He beckons IVAN to the table.

IVAN drops the knickers onto the mattress and goes over to sit next to FATHER.

FATHER gestures IVAN to eat.

Without looking, FATHER offers the knife to him, handle first.

IVAN takes the knife. He doesn't eat anything.

What is it? You didn't get any?

IVAN looks at FATHER silently.

Let you down, did he…? The bastard got his, and he didn't leave you any… My friend got shagged and all I got were these crusty knickers… Bet you've given them a sniff though, haven't you…? What the hell is it?

IVAN continues to sit in silence.

They stare at each other for a few moments.

You want some brandy?

IVAN: No, thanks. I'm taking medication.

FATHER: Fucking pills? Fuck 'em!

…

Well at least get me a brandy glass from the kitchen, please. It's on the tray…

IVAN puts the knife on the table, backs into the kitchen, and brings back a brandy glass

That's exactly it! If only the arsehole would do that occasionally… If he'd just try to help… Himself especially… The fuckwit… My dear Ivan, it's all gone to hell!

…

How's your mother?

IVAN: She's very well, thanks.

FATHER: Bollocks…! Stuck with you…? She was moaning on to me the other day about you dragging home some slapper.

IVAN: But… That's not true.

FATHER: I know it's not. Kidding, aren't I…? If only… But you can't be as mentally ill as she thinks you are… I told her – 'Let the lad get a bird, get his system all pumped out.'

…

I'm joking.

…

That said, though, she's been dragging you around these fucking doctors when it would have been better for you to visit a knocking shop. Cheaper too. Fuck me if *that* wouldn't sort your head out.

FATHER pours some brandy for himself, drinks.

You're sat there thinking, look who's talking, aren't you?

…

Thinking, if he had a fucking clue, he wouldn't be in this mess.

…

But your generation. You cunts ripped my heart out.

IVAN gets up.

IVAN: I'm sorry. I have to go now.

As IVAN exits, FATHER talks without looking at him. He carries on drinking.

FATHER: Go ahead, young man... Thank fuck for you... Keeping the house secure... My only friend in a sea of fuckwits.

IVAN has gone.

You're all I need when I feel like topping myself... Fuck it. Maybe you're sane and you're pissing yourself at the lot of us.

...

My wife gave me two lunatics, and I got the third free... Me... Gave the cow everything and she was still unhappy... 'Fucked her up', did I...? I dragged that peasant out of her fucking haystack... And now another lunatic's looking after my house... This place's gone to rack and ruin and he's 'looking after' it... Fucking cretin!

Knocking at the door.

Yes!

More knocking.

Let yourself in. I can't be arsed getting up.

DOOLE enters, followed by IGOR.

DOOLE: Afternoon, Uncle Jo.

IGOR: Good afternoon.

DOOLE: Well. Is Rasha here...? He's expecting us.

FATHER: I know you, do I?

DOOLE: Uncle Jo, it's me...Doole.

FATHER: Pleased to meet you... I'm Pozhunats, recovering alcoholic. Until I gave it up.

He shakes hands with DOOLE and then with IGOR. They are treating it as a joke.

FATHER is deadly serious.

Pozhunats, pleased to meet you…

IGOR: Igor, pleased to meet you.

…

You remember us, don't you, Uncle Jo…? I know I've not been around for ten years but –

FATHER: For all I know you *were* around, son, but I wasn't… Bugger ten years, I haven't been around for fifty! In fact, never… Now if you'll excuse me, I'll drain my bladder, if I may… I mean, this used to be my home, so if it's alright with you…

He goes to the toilet and carries on speaking while he urinates.

I'm talking crap, this never used to be my home.

…

Fuck it. Honestly, lads, I'm *trying* to be charming.

IGOR: Uncle Jo, do you remember – Rasha and me had our farewell party together? Before we went to the Army…? We were in the same unit too, until they sent him off to Slovenia.

…

I'm in England now.

…

I've lived there for ten years –

FATHER comes out, gets caught up in the curtain on the door.

FATHER: Which fucking idiot came up with this?

IGOR and DOOLE try to free FATHER.

Who lives in England?

IGOR: Me.

FATHER: Oh! It's you…! My Rasha got shipped to Slovenia to practice dodging shrapnel, and you stayed here…! Arranged by your old fella wasn't it? He's a slippier fucker than I am.

…

They never even told us when the motherfuckers moved him…! Two months we were waiting! Rasha, stuck in the fucking mud for sixty-three days.

…

You said you're living in England?

IGOR: Yes.

FATHER: Well fuck my old boots…! Good for you! Where? London?

IGOR: Near Leeds.

FATHER: Where near Leeds?

IGOR: Well I don't know how familiar you are with –

FATHER: Yorkshire! Lancashire! Northuumberland! Kent! I went there, son… In the Sixties. Was part of this dodgy industrial delegation…to Wales… The English tried to palm off some of their obsolete machinery on us – and this was when their cutting edge stuff was obselete itself, the crafty bastards… That's those fuckers to a tee, son… But the Welsh, now…! We were never bloody sober! Whole thing's a blank! The Welsh just kept saying 'Don't buy that shit, Tito boyo, it's no good for nothing!' Have to listen to the Welshman, he's been screwed by the English for centuries… This machinery. Fucking atrocious.

…

32

Swansea...! We went to Swansea!

...

The Welsh, yes... Great people... And you're in Leeds?

IGOR: Huddersfield. Or 'Oodersfield', as they say in
    Yorkshire...

FATHER: England's big. That's the truth...

IGOR: It's not *that* big –

FATHER: Are you fucking me about?

IGOR: No.

FATHER: England's immense, son, and you're fucking
    clueless... You think it's just what you can see, don't
    you? What about the islands? And the territories?
    England, my son, is fucking huge.

...

You couldn't fucking *conceive* of the size –

DOOLE: Where's Rasha, Uncle Jo?

FATHER: In England...

DOOLE and IGOR look at each other.

*FATHER goes over to the table, pours another glass and
drains it.*

DOOLE: Did he say when he was coming back? We'll
    come round later, shall we?

FATHER: It's fine! I'm off anyway... Sit yourselves down!
    Eat! Drink! Smoke...! I'm going... I've got things to do.
    Off on my usual crawl – 'The Ram's Head', 'The Rose',
    'The Marshal's Arms', 'The Rising Sun'... I'm a regular
    fucking regular...! Want to come...?

DOOLE: No, thanks... I'm in the car, though. I could drop you off somewhere...

FATHER: Well, that would be kind...! Used to have a car myself. I think I sold it this morning.

DOOLE: Okay...! Let's get going! Wait here Iggy? Rasha can't be long now.

IGOR: Yeah.

FATHER puts his coat on with DOOLE's help.

They start to leave.

FATHER turns towards the toilet again.

FATHER: Nice touch, that curtain... I owe whoever thought of that a drink...

DOOLE: Right, Uncle Jo. Where we off to, then?

FATHER: 'The Rose'! No, to 'The Marshal's Arms'! First 'The Marshal's Arms' and then 'The Rising Sun'...

DOOLE and FATHER go.

Igor is standing still. After a moment he goes to the curtain and straightens it.

So There You Go...

IGOR and RASHA are sitting at the table. MILLIE is lying on the mattress. MILLIE lights a joint which she and RASHA share.

RASHA: So there you go...Nada. Nobody left.

IGOR: Man, if there was one thing I missed, y'know... The gang....

IGOR gets up, stretches, walks slowly around the room.

RASHA: Truth hurts, Iggy. Still the truth though. All gone. Bunny's in Belgrade. Russki went and got married.

Couple of kids now… Want some?

IGOR: Not now.

…

What about your mum and your sister?

RASHA: Did you see my Dad? Hasn't got a fucking clue.
Not any more. *Boozum Delerio.*

…

She put a brave face on it to start with… Five years ago,
though, she'd had enough. Pissed off and took my sister
too.

…

Worked out alright. Mum got herself some geriatric
sugar daddy. Sister's at the Uni in Novi Sad.

IGOR: Fucked, that is. Your Dad used to be alright.

RASHA: Used to be. When they closed that fucking
factory it was like they'd taken his baby away. Used to
go on about his three children. Me, my sister and the
factory. How the factory was the child that fed us all.
Not healthy, is it?

…

Now he chucks me out and then he fucking panics 'cos
I'm not here.

…

Last year, it all got a bit much. I had to get the fuck out
for a few weeks… My Dad rang the police and said
'I need your help. My child's gone. Disappeared. My
child's been missing for a month…'

…

So the guy on the desk asks him for a description. Age, sex, distinguishing marks. That shit.

…

And my Dad says, 'Well, he's just turned thirty…'

RASHA starts laughing, chokes.

IGOR: And?

RASHA: They told him to fuck off!

MILLIE: Fucking cop! It's his fucking job to help, and he thinks he can just… Arrogant motherfucker…

RASHA: Calm down. Don't waste the weed.

MILLIE: Fuck you! Stop talking shit. It's hilarious, isn't it? He's crying out for help and all they can do is fuck him about! I can't believe you of all people think it's… treating someone in such a shitty way. You don't even find it funny anyway. Do you? You fucking liar.

…

Go on. Pretend to laugh. Then call an ambulance… The fucking cops. See what happens. Wait until you get sick. Until you're going under… Until –

MILLIE starts coughing. She puts her head in her hands and leaves it there.

For fuck's sake…

RASHA: This is why I stopped doing drugs… The older I get, the less I can keep up.

IGOR: How about the young lady?

MILLIE: Young lady?

MILLIE laughs.

Is that how everyone talks in England then?

IGOR: Hey. Just a figure of speech.

MILLIE gets up and turns to Igor.

MILLIE: Well the *young lady*'s so fucking battered that she can't speak like the BBC. Sorry.

RASHA: He's only asking Millie dearest. Come here... Let daddy kiss it better...

MILLIE stumbles through the curtain to the toilet.

We hear her retching.

IGOR: How old is she, man?

RASHA: Old enough. I'm helping her through *Hamlet.* For her exams.

IGOR: When did you graduate?

RASHA: Did I ever finish what I started?

IGOR: Well why don't you?

RASHA: I've forgotten where the fucking Uni is. Seriously.

...

Hardly left this room in five years.

IGOR: How d'you get by, then?

RASHA: On a steady diet of pain and bullshit... The odd article for the paper. Crappy literary magazines. Airing my views on local fucking radio.

IGOR: That's a living, man?

RASHA: You think anyone here's alive?

IGOR: Hey, you're seeing a lovely young lady. So you're alive!

MILLIE mumbles behind the curtain.

RASHA: No. I'm a hopeless fucking case.

...

And I'm not seeing her, I'm shagging her. Me Higgins, her Liza, yeah? The fucking porno Pygmalion. That's me, Iggy. Pedagogue to pretty girls. Or charming ones. Charming's enough.

...

You know where that word comes from? Charming? That's French. Describes a man's *feelings.* So obviously it's all about cock. Being so fucked and horny you couldn't care less. Any hole's a goal.

IGOR: Hey. It's all good.

RASHA: Why don't you stop that shit and tell me where you've been for eleven years?

...

Sit down and tell me a story, eh? No?

...

The house's fucked. The old fella's selling it off. Asset stripping. Fridge freezer, kitchen shelf, the complete works of Fyodor fucking Dostoyevsky. The door off the bog this morning... There's nothing upstairs... He took the heaters...

...

Soon be winter.

IGOR: Doole's on his way. Said he'd bring some beer.

RASHA: That shithead Doole's sold his soul.

IGOR: He's a real young professional. I don't quite understand what he's doing.

RASHA: Selling the big shit sandwich! Warehouse manager for some Swiss chocolate company. He's ballooning too. He's a fucking pig!

IGOR: At least he's got a bit of cash –

RASHA: Yeah, and that's another thing that gets on my tits. Never leaves the house of a weekend. Lying around in a pile of old memories and toblerone just farting and watching *The Simpsons.*

...

Pathetic.

IGOR: And you don't watch *The Simpsons*?

RASHA: (*Laughing.*) Don't have cable since my Dad sold the box. I'm holding onto the video by my fucking fingernails. That's it. Classic movies, porn and old school commie cartoons. Tell you what I fucking love, right? Me, a big fat joint and that shit. *The Stone Flower, The Tale of Tsar Zaltan, The Crippled Carthorse...* The Russians are amazing.

...

I mean *Grandad and the Magic Mushroom,* man! You can say that again... It's batshit! Sea monsters, witches, guys talking backwards, mutant little bastards with springs for legs. Jesus wept.

...

Millie, sweetie, are you alive?

MILLIE mumbles behind the curtain.

Poo poo! Wee wee! Sick it all up! Wash your face!

IGOR: I've often... I always thought you'd be striding around in some school. Torturing the kids with literary theory.

...

I was waiting for your first anthology.

RASHA: Poetry's dead, Iggy. Did that news never reach the real world?

IGOR: What?

RASHA: You've fucking forgotten? Think it was winter '95... All the papers ran a front page story. Seventy-two point glossy black type: 'Poetry est Morte!'...

IGOR: Poetry can't die.

RASHA: No shit? You should've said something.

IGOR: When was the funeral? What's the headstone like? Where's the grave?

RASHA: All around us.

IGOR: So that collection of yours never got published...

RASHA: Leave it.

...

I nearly wrote a book. An insider's view of the declining Slavic civilisation... The publisher was well up for it. In the end I couldn't be arsed.

IGOR: Why didn't you try?

RASHA: D'you think anyone really cares...? My view's not history. It's *anti*-history. A sprinkling of latent anti-semitism in there too – would've made the neonazis cream their fucking jeans... The faintest whiff of racism... Get this... The Slavs and the Germans are the same tribe, right? But the Germans always hated us because we never gave a fuck about the state, about order, about structure. That's why the Germans wanna wipe us out. You can't hate any cunt as much as you can hate your brother. Look at the national fucking emblems man. At the bottom line. The German eagle? One head. The Slav? Two. In their eyes, then, the Slav eagle's a fucking mutant. And this two headed Eagle? This unrealistic, *naturally impossible* symbol? Scares the Krauts shitless 'cos they're all bent out of shape by rationalism. They fear it the same way they fear imagination. And the Slav eagle *encapsulates* imagination. Your mono-cranial German eagle, fuck it. There it is flying around in the real world – there it is in the fucking zoo. You don't need to imagine it. Just pay your entrance fee and there it is. Beak, feathers and fucking cage.

...

And you know what man? They fucking managed it. I wanted to point out how the Slav religion, the Slav culture, *our fucking culture,* has basically been destroyed... All our proud, authentic pre-Christian rituals? Utterly extinct...

...

And the funny thing is – and those nazi cunts, they'll think this bit's hilarious – The Germans just tried to carry on what the Jews already started. Rewind, man. Just two thousand years or so. The Jews invented Christ, invented Christianity, to wind up the Romans. First a series of Romano-Christian conflicts, then a few centuries of Christianity spreading unchecked like a Rabbi-controlled virus... Eventually, though, they needed to wind the Christians up. What did they invent? Only fucking Islam...! The Eastern Christians reduced the Slavic wooden idols to ashes, the Greeks headed north to finish the half-arsed job the Romans made of fucking us up, and Prince Vladimir slaughtered most of the rest in the name of Jesus... The Byzantine Empire... Byzantium shattered the Slav spirit... The whole filthy fucking lot of them tore up our imagination

41

and spat on the pieces... The Anglo-Saxons, the Normans, the Celts, the Aboriginals, how come they all managed to preserve their old Gods, and we failed?

...

Because we're the kids in the European playground, man. We were, even before there was a Europe. We try and keep up with the big kids and copy every new game they bring along. And every few years, it's a new set of kids and a new set of rules. And we keep letting them kick our fucking heads in.

...

There you go. There are people out there who'd fucking *die* to publish that. Not that everybody would understand, of course... And I know all that anti-semitic stuff is fucking horseshit, but what can you do? It's the Slavic way... That's our bottom line, yeah? We have to have someone to blame... Essentially, we need a God, so let's create him!

IGOR: They wouldn't really publish that here?

RASHA: There'd be queues round the fucking block for it.

MILLIE comes out of the toilet. She looks pale.

And through it all the destruction of young healthy people goes on...

MILLIE: *Please.* Leave me out of this.

...

Fucking zombies.

MILLIE collapses onto the mattress.

RASHA: Let her sleep a bit... *Hamlet*'s fucking hard work... How did we ever put up with it, eh?

IGOR: School was great, man.

RASHA: Bollocks! *Tom Sawyer, Crime and Punishment, Quietly Flows the Don? Moby Dick...*? Used to send you insane. Too much to take in. You'd end up with the Cossacks chasing some Great White Whale up and down Old Mother Mississippi, and up pops T S fucking Eliot to do the newsflash...

IGOR: You took it all too seriously.

RASHA: Seriously, my arse. The only thing I ever respected – the only thing I still respect – the Pioneers' cap and scarf. That meant something. That was solidarity. Look at her... Stoned... Screwing around... D'you think she'd be in that state if she'd had to take the solemn oath of the Pioneers?

DOOLE comes in with a crate of beer.

DOOLE: 'Today as I become a Pioneer, I solemnly promise to defend...'

DOOLE puts the crate on the table, dishes out a can to each.

IGOR: Right on cue!

RASHA: Dickhead. That's the oath you made to the Yugoslav Army!

DOOLE: I never did time in the Yugoslav Army, mate. I did time in the Army of Yugoslavia...

RASHA: That's you all over you moron... Army of Yugoslavia? Then your Commander in Chief was fucking Milosevic, wasn't he? That's no army I was ever in. I served the people. Not that bastard Slobo.

IGOR: Right – so you're enemies now?

RASHA: I reckon... Why not?

...

Then we can exterminate each other.

DOOLE: Hey. Button it.

…

What's the matter with baby Jane?

RASHA: She's just diving for pearls. We'll all be fucked when she comes up for air again.

…

Cheers!

They toast each other.

DOOLE: Who is she?

RASHA: A Goddess.

DOOLE: Jesus, Rasha. Not another one of your kids?

RASHA: No. I'm telling you. The girl's a Goddess come to earth with spectacular tits and a pert ass. She's just paying us mortals a visit.

DOOLE: She's pretty.

RASHA: Beware her wrath, Doole.

DOOLE: I have to have a piss.

…

What's this?

RASHA: The curtain?

DOOLE: You're winding me up. Where's the door?

RASHA: Doors are dull, Doole.

DOOLE: Fair enough.

IGOR: Come on guys. I thought we were having fun.

DOOLE: (*While urinating.*) Yeah, well it's easy to have fun when you're raking in sterling, you fucker.

IGOR: Swap you?

...

RASHA: What do you do over there?

IGOR: I'm a lab technician. For a chemical company.

DOOLE: (*Coming out of the toilet.*) In Leeds?

IGOR: I work in Leeds, but I live in Huddersfield. 'Oodersfield', as they say in Yorkshire. We're planning to move to Leeds though.

DOOLE: Own flat and car?

IGOR: The car's mine. The flat's rented.

DOOLE: You've got a woman though?

IGOR: Yeah. I'm engaged.

...

Her name is Ana. She's Polish. And she's amazing.

RASHA: Catholic...

IGOR: Jewish, if it matters.

...

She's still at the Uni. We met there. She's a post-grad.

DOOLE: Man, I love Polish girls.

RASHA: How the fuck do you know what Polish girls are like?

DOOLE: Fine looking women...

RASHA: Doole, you'd say that about a ten euro an hour Albanian... You talk bollocks, but you'd never fucking empty them. At least not in a woman.

DOOLE: So I never shag?

RASHA: Look at yourself! Piling on the weight. Wanking yourself blind. Gorging on so much milk chocolate that your sperm are turning into cheese...

DOOLE: When Doole loves, he loves discreetly.

RASHA: Oh, come off it... You might as well varnish your cock and have done with it...

DOOLE: I had a shag.

...

I had a shag four hours ago.

RASHA: First time, was it?

DOOLE: An older woman, she was. Not bad either.

RASHA: Your Auntie's so good to you, isn't she?

DOOLE: She's a secretary. In the wholesale department. Been giving me the eye for weeks. You know?

...

Smiling.

RASHA: I can't believe it... Go on, tell more. You fucked a granny?

DOOLE: No.

...

She was forty-five. She was a vamp.

RASHA: And you were the virgin?

DOOLE: I was in her department. She says 'Stay for a coffee', so I did. Next thing I know, we're in her office and she's sucking me off...and I mean, this woman... been around the block, you know –

RASHA: So, Iggy, how's Huddersfield?

DOOLE: You don't believe me, do you, you cunt?

...

Well it fucking happened!

IGOR: Not much to tell. Like I said, planning to move to Leeds. Working. No free time. Mainly keep in touch with people by email. You got email?

DOOLE: I have. At work.

RASHA: Not me. It's for the best. My old man'd sell a computer for a sniff of fucking brandy.

IGOR: Oh, and I'm getting married next month.

DOOLE: That's fantastic.

RASHA: 'I'm getting married next month.' Fucking hell. Doesn't sound natural.

...

I mean planning things months in advance.

DOOLE: That's the way it works.

RASHA: What the fuck does that mean? 'That's the way it works?' You could be dead before next month over here. You can't make fucking plans.

DOOLE: You can. Get used to it Rasha. Times are changing.

RASHA: You crazy cunt.

DOOLE: We'll be like England one day. We're moving Westwards. Making concrete plans...

RASHA: Listen to yourself. You genuinely believe there'll be a knock on the door one day, don't you? You and the rest of the Economic Guinea Pigs. You think there'll be some bloke standing there... Good morning Mr Nestlé...! Thanks for all you effort, now here's your stock portfolio, your inflation-proof bank account... Kiss me you new minted capitalist... Can I finger your prostate? Blah. Blah. Fucking Blah –

IGOR: That doesn't happen anywhere.

RASHA: You think I've never told him that...? The Bolsheviks have had it, get it? The Reds have fucked off, all that's left are the cowardly fucking liberals who got sucked in by capital, and all the rest of us are scum. Peasants. The money's been and gone and he's still waiting, holding his bowl out.

DOOLE: I'm not waiting, I'm working. Working hard and putting some away –

RASHA: I'll tell you what your progress is. It's taking grannies up the arse at the back of the wholesale department!

DOOLE: What the fuck makes you think you can talk to me like that...? Have you actually moved in five fucking years? Have you made anything? You just wallow, and spew shite, and hate and –

RASHA: I don't hate anyone.

DOOLE: You're thirty years old man. How many days' work on file? None.

　　　...

Did you notice that law they passed? Get a job
tomorrow and you'll have to work til you're ninety
before they give you a fucking pension.

RASHA: As if there's going to be a fucking pension when
we're ninety. The world's going to fall apart by then you
stupid fuck.

DOOLE: Oh well we'd all like to sit around spouting
amateur philosophy...

RASHA: Come on, Igor, tell him they broke the world!
Tell him it's not worth the stress because that's how it is!

IGOR: Well, the world *has* gone to shit.

...

But there's no reason not to drink to that.

They clink cans, then drink.

MILLIE wakes up, holds her hand to her mouth.

RASHA gets up.

RASHA: What is it, love?

RASHA takes her behind the curtain, MILLIE vomits.

IGOR: Let's not fight.

...

I only wanted to have a laugh. Relax a bit.

DOOLE: I'm sorry. But I work, you know. I fucking try. I
don't enjoy having the piss taken –

IGOR: Give him a hand.

DOOLE: Me? Why don't you? You're the one who's got it
made, Iggy. Why don't you solve the bastard's problems
for him?

IGOR: It's not a question of –

...

Listen, man, as soon as I've sorted the paperwork for the wedding, I'm out of here. I'd stay if I could, but... Doole. You're here.

...

You watched this happen.

...

He should be living on his own. It'd do him good. His Dad's crushing him, Doole. He's...screwed.

DOOLE: You're wrong man. He fucking loves it. His theory's that everything's 'falling apart'. If he's in a situation where everything *is* – it supports his theory. QED.

...

IGOR: Keeps him rooted?

DOOLE: Yeah. It was so near to being different. But there was all that shit five years ago. His parents. It...deflated him. Then he had all the other disappointments. He had a girlfriend. Same girl for almost six years. I mean that's a long time. He was at Uni. They were living together. Wanted a job so he could stay with her. All that. Only gave a fuck about her. Not his parents. Not anyone. He was even writing for some literary mag. He was on the staff, paying his rent, making it fucking work...

IGOR: And?

DOOLE: It all went to shit. The economy. The fucking politics. Times were harder than they are now, Iggy. People stopped giving a fuck about poetry and started worrying about survival. You know what it was like, back then.

IGOR looks at DOOLE. Shrugs.

...

DOOLE laughs.

IGOR: And the girlfriend?

DOOLE: Things end. It ended. He came back, and he's still here.

...

Still fucked up about it.

IGOR: Harder to roll with the punches when you're thirty.

DOOLE: I thought he was stronger than that.

IGOR: So what about the kid?

DOOLE: Masochism.

...

Oh shit, I don't know

...

He finds one, it fucks up, he finds another. He thinks he's teaching them about life. Truth is they're the only people he can feel spiritually superior to.

...

Give me an older woman any day. Last thing they want is commitment.

IGOR: Everyone struggles to commit.

DOOLE: Jesus, Iggy, that's the same shite he comes out with. Like, 'people have lost their concentration, they're deaf and blind to the world', blah blah blah...

RASHA comes out from behind the curtain. He takes MILLIE towards the mattress.

RASHA: I wouldn't go in there for a bit, guys.

...

Come on sweetie, bedtime...

RASHA puts MILLIE down on the mattress.

She reaches up and locks her hands behind his neck.

MILLIE: Rasha. You lie down with me. I told Mum and Dad I was staying at Anita's.

RASHA gently extricates himself from MILLIE.

She falls back onto the mattress.

He rejoins the others.

RASHA: God, she's lovely, isn't she?

DOOLE: We know what you think.

RASHA: I'm going to clean up in there. Then I'm gonna play you fuckers some really good music! Really fucking good! Give us that beer...

RASHA takes the can, a big gulp, and disappears behind the curtain.

'Like A Hurricane'

IGOR, DOOLE and RASHA are sitting at the table, enthusiastically eating kebabs. MILLIE is sitting on the mattress, eating off a plate. The table is covered with cans and glasses. In the background Neil Young's unplugged version of 'Like a Hurricane' plays on a loop.

IGOR: Neil Young!

DOOLE: For the fifth time in a row.

RASHA: And at least five times more!

IGOR: This kebab's amazing!

DOOLE: Delicious.

IGOR: Could do with a bit of ketchup though.

RASHA jumps up off the chair.

RASHA: Ketchup I can do.

RASHA quickly goes into the kitchen and comes back with a bottle of ketchup. He puts it on the table.

They continue eating.

DOOLE: Where are we up to?

IGOR: First desk on the middle row.

DOOLE: The Radyenovich girl! Married. One kid. Husband's a copper. Used to sit with...

IGOR: Don't tell me! What was her name?

...

Rasha?

RASHA: As if I give a fuck about that bunch of cretins.

DOOLE: Got it. Yasna Pavkovich! She's a secretary at the city council. Her Dad sorted the job out. As yet, unmarried.

RASHA: Like that dog'd ever get married.

IGOR: Next... Yakshich and Vladan!

DOOLE: Yakshich died in Kosovo.

IGOR: Fucking hell!

DOOLE: Special forces. Blown up.

IGOR: Oh fuck...

DOOLE: During the bombing, as I recall. Bumped into him a month before. He's wheeling along a pushchair with his kid in it. 'You're not down there? – I ask him. 'No, bro,' he says – 'But I'm going back, and believe me, we'll fucking fuck them, every single one of those fucking NATO fuckers!' I look at him. I look at the kid. And I'm thinking 'You know what the chances of me going there'd be? With a kid like that?'

RASHA: Serbia's full of orphans. Orphans and kebabs!

IGOR: Shit...

DOOLE: Well they sure made kebabs out of Yakshich!

IGOR pushes his plate away.

Then... Vladan! He's in the States. IT engineer. Think he's with IBM... Behind those two – Savich and Stepanov. Savich went abroad too, I heard she married a Frog... Stepanov's got a fruit stall... Kostich is working with his dad, designing business cards and doing black market software... Pinter. Now he was inside for two years – he was working at the fish farm and selling knock-off fish to the fishmongers at night so they did him for unlawful possession. He's at the green market now hawking some Hungarian shit...

MILLIE: It's not the worst thing you could do.

DOOLE: No it isn't. But these are the people who went through the shit with us. It's important. You'll understand.

...

In about ten years.

MILLIE: I understand now. It's hardly an epic saga of tragic proportions, is it?

RASHA gives the ketchup bottle a shake and accidentally sprays DOOLE's shirt.

DOOLE: Fucking hell, man! That's my best fucking shirt...! It's Italian! Do you know how much this cost...? Seventy fucking Euros! Half my wages!

DOOLE runs to the toilet.

We hear running water.

IGOR looks uncomfortable.

RASHA laughs.

We hear DOOLE behind the curtain.

Stop fucking laughing!

...

It's gonna fucking stain! I know it!

MILLIE: You better fuck off home and put it in the machine.

RASHA laughs even more loudly. He takes the ketchup bottle, squeezes it all over himself.

DOOLE comes out of the toilet with no shirt on. He looks at RASHA and bursts out laughing.

They all laugh.

IGOR: My fucking fault. I would ask for ketchup...

RASHA puts the music up.

IVAN enters cautiously.

RASHA beckons him to come in, turns the music down again.

RASHA: Guys, meet the resident genius! This is Ivan! A poet! A spiritual seeker! Come in Ivan. Sit down. Help yourself!

MILLIE: Just in time Ivan. We were beginning to think the Messiah would never come.

IVAN: Actually my mother sent me.

...

She says can you turn the music down, please.

RASHA: Just been done. What's going on?

IVAN: Nothing... I've been reading.

RASHA: For the purposes of relaxation?

IVAN: I don't know.

RASHA: Go back, check everything's cool with your Mum, and come and join us, okay? Tell her we've put the music down a bit too.

IVAN: Okay.

IVAN goes out.

MILLIE: What did you tell him to come back for? *Join us?* Join what for fuck's sake? Three pissed morons, sitting around having a laugh at his expense?

IGOR: What's his problem?

DOOLE: You don't remember Ivan?

IGOR: Where from?

DOOLE: He was in our year... Went to the Tech. The judo champ. He twatted those ten coppers...

IGOR: Not sure...

RASHA: Amazing guy. White wizard, yogic expert, mystic...

IGOR: I might –

RASHA: He's dropped about twenty kilos.

...

He's got an artificial hip...

IGOR: Fuck, yes! That's never him? He doesn't look like himself.

RASHA: How could he? After a decade in and out of the nuthouse?

MILLIE: Tell me he's not coming back...

RASHA: Sweetie. He's our old friend. From school...

IGOR: How the hell did that happen?

RASHA: What can you do, Ig? We were mental when you left us. How d'you think we are now? I'll get him to explain.

DOOLE: What needs explaining?

RASHA: He can tell us his life story...

MILLIE: Oh no.

RASHA: I agree sweetie. It's pretty fucking rough.

DOOLE: He'll never tell us.

...

Guys like that. They don't...to strangers...

RASHA: So I'll introduce you. Let's have a laugh... He's written a shitload of poems too. I'm just trying to find him a publisher...

Laughter.

RASHA: Don't fucking laugh... He's a great writer.

IGOR: What's...medically wrong with him?

RASHA: He's a neurotic.

DOOLE: That's not an illness, man. We're all neurotic.

RASHA: It's an illness for him. He's scared of everything.

IGOR: Fear of fear.

RASHA: Exactly... We'll kill the music when he gets back... Skin up, darling. It's gonna be mad.

MILLIE: It's a long way past mad you idiot.

DOOLE: I don't believe it.

IGOR: What's the matter now?

DOOLE: I've got to have some sweets.

RASHA: Good idea that man! Go. Fetch KitKat.

DOOLE: I will! Shit. I'm going to miss the start...

DOOLE leaves quickly.

RASHA: We'll have to ease him into it. And make sure you listen. It's important to him.

...

He doesn't make eye contact when he talks, right? And when you talk to him, he stares at the floor...

IGOR: He's not violent, is he?

RASHA: Is he fuck! He's as gentle as they come.

...

Now you'll see what the machine did to us, man. That, and what's left.

IVAN enters.

Sit down mate! You know Millie, right?

MILLIE: Hello Ivan. You know Rasha? Right?

RASHA: And this is my old friend Igor.

...

Want some kebab?

IVAN: Thanks. No.

RASHA: You don't smoke weed, do you...? Ketchup? (*Laughs.*) Except all the ketchup we had's all over me. (*He laughs.*) ...Smoke?

IVAN: I can't.

RASHA: Fair enough, we'll do the smoking and you just enjoy yourself.

...

Iggy might be interested in publishing your book.

IVAN: Mhm.

RASHA: I told him about your poetry. How much I believe in it. He's agreed to front us the money, no problem. The only thing is –

...

Look, you can tell we trust each other, can't you? Thing is, Igor's interested in... Fascinated by... Your case history, Ivan.

...

When did you start to feel afraid?

IVAN: You really want me to talk about it?

RASHA: If you can. Everything you've ever told me. The relevant contexts, the therapy. The feelings. The things you did to help the time pass...

IVAN: Everything?

RASHA: Sure! I'll help you. Ivan can't talk for a... sustained length of time. He gets tired quickly. Give us what you can, and I'll help you. I'll fill in... Okay?

IVAN: Okay.

RASHA: When did it all start?

RASHA and IGOR are smoking and drinking beer.

MILLIE is sipping wine. From time to time they try to stifle laughter and sometimes they are very serious.

IVAN talks earnestly. He keeps cracking his knuckles.

IVAN: It was May. The May that I was twelve years old. My Father was still living with us, but we weren't in the place we're in now. I was on the balcony and suddenly the fear came over me. I couldn't tell what was real... and what wasn't. My imagination, it...it caught fire...

RASHA: Was it the height?

IVAN: A small part of it.

   ...

But it was more...an inexplicable fear. Of everything, and from everywhere. All of a sudden I was pale, sweaty. My Mother...she pulled me back inside. It took me a few days to recover.

   ...

I read a lot. At the time I was mainly reading medical encyclopedias –

RASHA: You could say you read excessively?

IVAN: I suppose. It was the morbid fear of sharp objects that came next. And then...they just accumulated. After that it was open spaces.

RASHA: At what age?

IVAN: Sixteen.

RASHA: Which was when you started on the yoga manuals?

IVAN: Yes... On my seventeenth birthday, I contracted the fear of insanity. But I still kept reading the yoga books. I read everything about... I wanted to know it all –

RASHA: And you used to have your own teacher, yes?

IVAN: True. He helped me transcend some of the phobias. I applied all my learning through meditation. I was... under his guidance. My eighteenth birthday was coming up. I subsequently developed a fear of women. I had a huge...a need for their company. But the terror of intimacy. It overrode it.

RASHA: And suddenly...

IVAN: Suddenly all my fears vanished...just...gone.

...

I started to read texts on the occult. The Kabbalah, specifically. On a practical level I was carrying out visualisation exercises. With imaginary objects in a space. Yoga, Kabbalah, they came really easily. It was the judo, you see. I was stronger then, more flexible, I was completely at home in my body.

RASHA: Were there elements of...black magic?

IVAN: No! I swear to God. Only white magic. I knew of... certain people who were using the inverted pentagram, but I never –

RASHA: Who was?

IVAN: You know this.

…

I told you all about it.

RASHA: It was your yoga teacher.

IVAN: Yes.

RASHA: Tell them how you found him out, Ivan. Wasn't his name Goran?

IVAN: Goran…yes. During one particular lesson, I noticed a drawing. In the exercise room

RASHA: Where, exactly?

IVAN: On the floor. Blended in so skilfully, it was almost impossible to spot. An inverted pentagram…

RASHA: What was this Goran trying to do?

IVAN: He was trying to attach larvae to my aura. But I was stronger than he was.

RASHA: What kind of larvae?

IVAN: Some people create negative larvae and try to stick them to other people's auras. If you let them, they attach themselves. They're parasitical. They suck out the energy…your good energy. Your positive energy. If you're strong enough, though, your aura's impenetrable, They just die. Or they move on to somebody weaker.

…

And after that I went off to do my National Service.

RASHA: But prior to that?

IVAN: I don't know.

RASHA: Ten policemen? At the same time?

IVAN: That was… I wouldn't want to talk about that.

RASHA: Then I'll do it...! Ivan discovered the location of a secret masonic meeting. He tried to break in while they were performing their ritual. The police headed you off though, didn't they? Started beating you too. Didn't they, Ivan?

...

That's right, isn't it?

IVAN: I wanted to break in... I wanted to expose them.

RASHA: Where was the meeting?

IVAN: In a school.

RASHA: Which one?

...

It's okay. I know you won't tell us... We'll have to live in ignorance. Could have been our school, eh, Iggy?

IGOR: Could have been anywhere...

DOOLE enters with the biscuits, panting.

RASHA goes over to him.

DOOLE: Did I miss anything?

RASHA: You missed what you missed. KitKat! Now!

DOOLE and RASHA investigate the sweets

MILLIE: You really live in England, don't you?

IGOR: I guess I do.

MILLIE: Jesus. A real Englishman. Just look at you.

...

So why'd you come back?

IGOR looks at DOOLE and RASHA. Shrugs. Smiles.

IGOR: This is where I'm from.

RASHA: Jesus Christ, Doole! This is Turkish fucking
Delight! Could you honestly not tell the difference?

DOOLE: It's good enough! Stop your whining and pass
me a beer.

RASHA: They'll never let you run Nestlé at this rate,
dickwad! Not if you can't tell the difference between…
Did you get distracted by the old woman behind
the counter? Was that it? You'd buy any old shit off
a Granny, wouldn't you…? I'm going to buy you a
fucking KitKat and staple it to the front of your Eye-
talian shirt! Would that help you remember?

DOOLE: Leave it.

RASHA: Leave it? KitKats have wafers in! Wafers! You
cunt.

DOOLE: What did I miss?

IGOR: Be quiet. You'll pick it up.

RASHA: Sorry, Ivan… You carry on. Sorry… This is
Doole, a fucking gerontophile who doesn't know what a
KitKat is.

…

What was the army like?

IVAN: Well, my health deteriorated. I was in the toughest
programme…

RASHA: The Special Forces training, yeah?

IVAN: Yes. Because of the judo. Back then I was twenty
kilos heavier too…

RASHA: How long did you last?

IVAN: The induction and then another two months. But then. Insomnia. I withdrew from everyone. Wouldn't communicate, so they sent me for therapy. After that they discharged me. I was sedated for the next six months, effectively. Couldn't even get out of the house. The pills were too…heavy. Couldn't read. Couldn't think, even… I'm sorry. I'm getting a bit tired…

RASHA: I understand. You want a beer?

IVAN: No. If there's any coffee though, I'd –

RASHA: Go on, Millie. Put some coffee on!

MILLIE: Do what?

RASHA: Coffee. Ivan wants some coffee.

MILLIE: That's it?

RASHA: For fuck's sake! Move your arse! Do something useful.

MILLIE: Why don't *you* move your arse and do something useful? Fuck this!

RASHA: Fuck what? Now *you* need something too?

MILLIE: Yeah. I need you to go and fuck yourself. (*To RASHA, quietly.*) Instead of screwing him.

MILLIE goes to the kitchen.

RASHA: Great. Now I'm getting shit off a teenager on top of everything else.

…

I'm sorry, Ivan.

…

What medication was it?

IVAN: 'Meleryl'. It suppresses the libido too...

RASHA: Doole should take that one. For the sake of
grannies everywhere....

IVAN: Then, 'Leogenretard' – Twenty-four hours of 'calm
and collected' thinking at a time, that one.

...

My muscles atrophied... At nineteen I was admitted to
hospital. In Belgrade... They told me to stop reading.
No yoga, no Kabbalah. Definitely no tarot... For the next
seven or eight years I was just...medicated. Four hundred
and seven milligrammes a day... Obviously they
changed some of the dosages over time. Tried out new
approaches...

IVAN thinks for a moment, then continues, brightly.

You, know, they even decreased it once or twice...

*DOOLE, IGOR and RASHA are looking at each other. They
try to suppress the laughter caused by the weed and beer, aware
that it goes against what they've heard. They all look at IVAN.
A moment of silence, then they piss themselves laughing.*

IGOR: This is fucking awful!

DOOLE: They ruined him. He's broken!

RASHA: Four hundred and seven milligrams! For all this
fucking time! Someone should go to prison!

DOOLE: Why didn't they give him a girl when he was
seventeen!

RASHA: Fuck! Why didn't they give him a granny?

IGOR: Even... Oh Jesus... Even cod liver oil!

DOOLE: I wonder... Round here... How many other
cases!

RASHA: God knows!

DOOLE: You're the tip of the fucking iceberg!

RASHA: Sorry Ivan, we're so fucking stoned. I'm out of control…

IGOR: Guys. Really, It's not fucking funny!

They are crying with laughter.

DOOLE: I'm gonna piss myself!

RASHA: Me too!

MILLIE brings in a cup of coffee and gives it to IVAN.

DOOLE: That's it. He'll be cured when he's had a coffee!

IGOR: He'll be resurrected!

RASHA: Hey. Cut it out. Stop it!

Eventually, they calm down.

Sorry, Ivan… This is ridiculous… What the fuck's the matter with you two?

DOOLE: Us?

RASHA: The guy's mortified…

IGOR: 'Mortified' is possibly an understatement…

They calm down. Suddenly, their full attention is on IVAN.

IVAN: For seven or eight years the uppermost idea in my mind was the centrality of reincarnation to the essence of life… I worked in a factory for three or so years. Heavy industry. Then I had a pretty serious accident. They had to put an artificial hip in me. I had to go on disability. No option really.

…

I live with my mother. And now I'm thirty years old. I had an orthodox baptism. That was only three years ago, and these days I'm only on sedatives. Just the five milligrammes of Haloperidol. Helps with psychosis too. Oh, and five milligrammes of 'Artan' to combat the stiffness. I take pleasure in walking. I have a friend. Walk to his place and back every day... You can keep that book I gave you, Rasha...

RASHA: Neil Sorski?

IVAN: That's it.

RASHA: And what does Father Neil say?

IVAN: Well St Anthony the Great says: 'Believe deep inside that this day is your last...'

RASHA jumps up, surprising the others, who are stoned, half asleep, or both.

RASHA: Isn't he sensational? Look! The Great Father Ivan! Yogi! Alchemist! Kabbalist...! You see how steep the path to true faith is? The many pitfalls? How much you have to let them screw you around? Four hundred and seven milligrammes a day! For that long! I wouldn't be surprised if God asked you to pray for *him* after all that shit! Behold the distance this man's travelled! Nowhere! Utterly, wholly ruined. Physically *and* psychologically... But at least his poetry's fantastic.

...

I'm joking.

...

Fuck it, Ivan, at least your God's convenient. At least he fits in the palm of your fucking hand...! Go on, Ivan! Reveal him to us!

RASHA grabs hold of IVAN roughly, shakes him, forcefully goes through his pockets – prayer beads and some tablets. He holds the tablets up.

Aha! Here he is! And God has a name! 'Ha-lo-pe-ri-dol'! What a good name for a deity! 'Haloperidol'! Like, 'hallo – here I am – I'm your God'! And how doth he manifest himself? Well he's round, porous and small. Fucking miniscule, in fact, but a God all the same! There he is, eh? Your tiny Saviour! It couldn't. Be fucking. Simpler.

IVAN puts down his coffee cup and leaves quietly.

Everybody is sombre, apart from RASHA.

He is very drunk and increasingly restless.

What the fuck is it with you people...? Enjoying yourselves?

IGOR: You've fucked it, man... What the hell did you do to him?

RASHA: Give me a break. We're mates...

DOOLE: Seriously. You've seriously fucked the guy up... Talking all that shit.

RASHA: What the fuck would you two know? I spend every day hauling him out of the fucking mire! Half an hour of his crap and you fell for it...! Half an hour! He's sick, you fucks! Possessive! Clings on to me for dear fucking life... I talk to him more than his own Mother does!

...

Wait till tomorrow... He'll be round here at the crack of dawn with some idea about the sanctity of worship. 'The demon envies the man who prays earnestly...' I'm not going to lose any sleep and neither's he!

...

But I guess I've royally pissed you off. Should I make it up to you? Eh? Well check this out, fuckers.

RASHA leaves, and returns wearing the Pioneer's cap with the red star and a red scarf around his neck.

Ta-da! Hey? Wankers!!! What about your oath? 'I give my word of honour as a Pioneer', eh!?

DOOLE and IGOR thaw out a bit, take a can each, laugh at RASHA.

DOOLE: Come on, drink… We've not seen the guy for ten years and we're upsetting him.

IGOR: Let's have a drink. Yeah.

RASHA: Go on, Mill. Put that tape on. Let's have a laugh.

MILLIE: Which tape?

RASHA: 'Hot Home Movie Fucking Volume One', baby!

MILLIE: Fuck off! That's between us, you fucking moron. Not your mates. Just us!

RASHA: Hey! These are my oldest fucking friends…give it here!

MILLIE lunges toward the video recorder but RASHA pushes her away.

MILLIE: No! Really, I'll go fucking mental. I swear! I'll scream!

RASHA grabs hold of her, twists her arm, covers her mouth with his hand.

While MILLIE is kicking in vain, RASHA manages to press the play button on the video.

Panting can be heard.

DOOLE and IGOR look on, stunned.

DOOLE: What's this?

IGOR: I don't…

MILLIE, sobbing, slides to the floor and lies in front of RASHA.

DOOLE: Jesus, I recognise him…

RASHA: How about the woman?

DOOLE: Looks familiar too…

RASHA: Welcome back to small town life, Iggy. Everyone knows everything, everyone, everywhere…

DOOLE: Fucking hell… It's that lawyer, isn't it? Him and his wife… Where did you get this from?

RASHA: Fucked her, have you?

MILLIE jumps up, hysterical. She grabs the cassette out of the video, yanks the tape out of the cassette.

MILLIE: Cunt! Fucking wanker!

MILLIE slaps RASHA, runs out.

RASHA: That was her Mum and Dad.

IGOR: Rasha.

…

What did you play that for?

DOOLE: This is…unbelievable… I'm going, man…

DOOLE, resigned, gets up and starts to go.

RASHA: Fuck you then. The world's going to shit, and what's your answer? Leave. Turn your back on us. Go on, you uncaring fucker. Pure as the driven snow, aren't you, until some granny grabs your cock…

DOOLE: That's it, man. Too fucking much… I'm… nauseous…

RASHA: We're all sick, Doole….

DOOLE: Well what the fuck do you want from me? You pontificating cunt. You fucked up, is that it? What is it with you? Do you only stop hating yourself when you've got a victim? What the fuck are you trying to do you spiteful little arsehole? Stage managing your little scenes –

RASHA: Well at least you're paying attention.

DOOLE: Oh yeah. 'Society's got ADHD, man. People need this. People need that. People need focus.'

…

Change the fucking record, won't you?

RASHA: And how long have you lasted, then? Nobody listens, you self-satisfied cunt! Nobody sees! It's all flashes. Scribbles. Unfinished sentences. Kids scrawling on the fucking toilet walls. What, precisely, is the function of this conversation, Doole?

DOOLE: I don't know… There isn't –

…

I'm going.

RASHA: Exactly. You're going. Where? I don't give a fuck. What have we talked about? Who gives a fuck? Who are we? We don't give a fuck. And nobody, but nobody gives a fuck about what he's been doing in Yorkshire for the last ten years. Who gives a fuck if he's moving to Leeds or whether he's screwing some Polack?

IGOR: Okay. Okay you're right…

IGOR is the closest to being sober. He tries to stay cool, drinking his beer slowly.

RASHA: We're zip! Zero! Four hundred and seven

milligrammes a day each, give it a couple of years, and then ask us what's important! We're the worms that got clever! We screw on, eating the mud, shitting the mud, eating the shit, screwing the shit, until you've shat out your own brain and it's just a pile of tangled images and sounds and then it's over and excuse me, but what the fuck was all that about? Scrape together thirty seconds of meaning out of life and then make me a fucking advert!

DOOLE: I can't listen to... I'm genuinely sorry we have to part like this...

RASHA: Pathos, now, is it...

DOOLE: I'm tired. I'm tired and I've got to be in work early... Iggy...

DOOLE goes.

IGOR: Wow... Looks like we've all overdone it a bit tonight eh...? I reckon once a decade's enough. Maybe even a bit too much.

IGOR gets up.

Don't envy you, Rasha. Having to tidy this place up.

IGOR smiles, shakes his head.

It's the way it goes, isn't it? Had all these things I wanted to say, man, but I guess it never goes like you expect it to.

IGOR prepares to leave.

RASHA: Iggy?

...

How did you spend the last ten years?

IGOR: It flew by, man. But I got a lot done, you know?

...

You?

RASHA: It flew by man. But I've done nothing.

...

You know?

IGOR: Don't.

...

I hope you don't think... But Doole told me. Your tragic love story.

RASHA stares at IGOR. His eyes well up.

RASHA: Five years, seven months, twenty two days... It was a cathedral, you know...? And now... I took so much care. Designing it. Building it. And then, between us. We blew the fucker up. There's not a more beautiful ruin anywhere... They should do sightseeing trips, Iggy. Fucking coach parties...

He lets his tears roll down his face...

And it'll always be there. It'll never wash away.

IGOR: When it rains in Huddersfield, in that boring way it does. Sometimes... Always when I'm on my own in the house... I start thinking...it's sad, but I start thinking, 'What a horrible place...' A grey valley filling up with grey rain. And then I think...

...

Back there it was never as grey as this. In my head, here. It's sunny.

RASHA: There you go. Sunny as Huddersfield is in mine...

IGOR: It's over in Huddersfield. I told you. We're moving to Leeds...

RASHA: Huddersfield... What the fuck is there in Huddersfield anyway?

IGOR: Rain. Wind.

He laughs.

You know what sticks in my head about Huddersfield...? They've got this lion.

RASHA: A lion...? A real lion?

IGOR: A sculpture of a lion.

RASHA: A sculpture?

IGOR: Didn't notice it for days. I only saw him the first time I was in a tall building.

RASHA: You didn't notice a fucking lion?

IGOR: He's standing on the roof of a building, man.

RASHA: Why?

IGOR: He's just standing. Proud. Looking out.

RASHA: What's he looking at?

IGOR: Not much. Just the town. This white stone lion. It captivated me. Made me happy in a weird way...

RASHA: Cheered you up?

IGOR: Yeah. Took me back to the city gardens. That stone lion's still sleeping there, isn't it?

RASHA: Yeah.

IGOR: Why did we love it? When our parents used to take us there? Because they used to let us sit on him. Right on the lion's back. I've still got a photo. Me as a kid. Sitting on the back of a sleeping lion, man...

RASHA: I've got one too. You and me on a sleeping yellow lion.

IGOR: Well that's what I remembered, over there. Except the lion in Huddersfield, it's white.

RASHA: And ours is yellow… Give us anything, you can bet we'll piss on it…

IGOR: I need to sleep. I'll have to go, Rasha…

RASHA: Shit…! That's it! The only good idea that wanker Prince of Denmark ever had. Almost patriotic… I never told the kid about his idea…about Fortinbras and his fucking armies… That's the *key*! Turks! Mongols! Whoever! Get it? Foreign rule promotes cohesion… Solidarity against invaders! Good for the birth rate. Good for the spiritual life too – Slaves, breeding themselves to victory… This shit…it's important…

IGOR gets up and goes.

RASHA is looking aside, drinking his beer.

Huddersfield…

The Witching Hour

Night. It's dark in the lounge. A faint light coming from the toilet. RASHA is asleep on the mattress. A shadow by the table. As he approaches the light, IVAN can be made out in the darkness.

IVAN: I tried to help… Everything I could… Not with a false face either. Not maliciously… Not like you. You're hurtful, Rasha. You're hurtful and you're a liar.

…

Today was a trial. A test. The hardest test. It seemed to come from nowhere, but it didn't. You laid the trap, Rasha. You took your mask off. Couldn't resist it, could you? Spewing out your thoughts until I saw them all before me… I know it all now. All the falsehoods.

…

76

I could forgive you those...the lies. I could forgive you those, but I can't forgive your determination to lead me off the path. The satanic traps you laid. You're Goran in a new form. A servant of the same master. Just a servant... My manuscripts...gone. Ashes. What do I need them for? I didn't write them, not really. *Tempter.* Encourager of weakness. You wanted it from me, didn't you? A little honest faith and some spiritual peace. Well here it is. Don't pretend you don't know what I mean, Rasha... This ends now, and it ends by my hand. It's fated. Predestined... Goran made sure of that... I prayed for him, I truly did, and I truly loved him... And you work alongside him... From inside him... I know you're awake. That you're listening. Demons like you, they don't rest, they don't sleep...

IVAN comes closer to the mattress. He is carrying a large knife.

RASHA moves in his sleep.

God, forgive me...

RASHA: Jesus. What now...? Who's that...?

IVAN: Judgement.

RASHA: Ivan, is that you...? What's up...?

IVAN: Reckoning...

RASHA: What...? Jesus, Ivan, what's got into you? That's a fucking big knife, man...

IVAN bends over RASHA and stabs him violently, several times.

RASHA cries out silently, and is still.

IVAN covers RASHA's body with a blanket.

A Wake Up Call

RASHA is lying on the mattress, in his clothes, dead to the world. FATHER enters , stumbling drunk. He stumbles over to RASHA. Looks at him. He's surprised.

FATHER: Rasha?

...

Son?

He bends down and grabs RASHA, who is still covered in ketchup.

FATHER lets go of him, starts sobbing, looks at his ketchup covered hands.

FATHER: Rasha! Rasha! Those fucking motherfuckers!

RASHA wakes up with a start, mumbles in disapproval, props himself up on his hands.

FATHER: Rasha, who did this to you, son? Who...? Tell me!

RASHA: Dad? Tell you what?

FATHER: Where did all this blood come from?

RASHA gets up, swaying with a hangover.

RASHA: Ketchup... Dad, it's only ketchup...

FATHER is speechless. He slowly brings his fingers up to his face. Sniffs them. Pause. Tastes them. Pause. Suddenly he slaps RASHA across the face.

RASHA falls to the floor.

FATHER: You motherfucker! You're trying to finish me off, aren't you? You wanna give me a coronary? Motherfucker! I'm going to the fucking police... I mean it! I'm gonna tell them you're trying to do me in...

You'll fucking go down for this. Prison! That's where you're going, soon as they get here...!

FATHER hurries out.

RASHA gets up. Goes over to the table and sits down. He strokes the place where FATHER hit him.

A knock at the door.

RASHA doesn't respond.

The door opens slowly.

We hear IVAN.

IVAN: Rasha?

...

Rasha...? It's me...

Still no response.

IVAN comes in tentatively. Under his arm is a wooden sculpture. The sculpture is rough, childish. It appears to be the head of a woman with braided hair and her mouth open as if is yawning or shouting. IVAN comes in, puts the sculpture on the table, and sits down.

Rasha. I need to tell you something. What I've been thinking about. It's over, you know? All of it. I'm never going to find a girl. Don't even know why I try. Won't be having a family. Children. I can see all of that now.

...

And I...really like your girlfriend. She's so pretty, and you're a handsome guy, too, Rasha. And smart. And you should have somebody. Everybody should. And if I did something wrong last night, I'm sorry. I need to say that. To apologise to you, your friends, and your girlfriend. Millie. Is that right?

RASHA: Yeah. Millie.

IVAN: Pass on my sincere apologies to her. Please.

RASHA: I fucked it up Ivan. I really, really fucked it up.

RASHA doesn't move.

IVAN: Do you need some time alone…? Sorry…

IVAN slowly goes to the door.

RASHA: Last night. I dreamed about you…

IVAN: You dreamed about me?

RASHA: I'm so fucking sorry, Ivan…

RASHA starts crying. He shakes uncontrollably and screws his face up.

Please forgive me…

IVAN: Is everything…? Shall I fetch you something? Something to calm you down…?

RASHA lays his hands on the table, puts his head down and continues to cry more and more loudly.

IVAN comes over to him and puts his hand on RASHA's shoulder.

A good cry can be a…positive thing… Just carry on… I'm here…

RASHA raises his head. He sees the sculpture on the table. He looks at it for a long time.

That? It's some of my art. I brought it round to show you…

RASHA stops crying, wipes his face on his sleeve.

RASHA: It's one of yours?

IVAN: Is it that obvious?

...

I've never seen anything uglier in my life...

RASHA laughs and IVAN joins him, even louder.

RASHA: So. This masterpiece. What does it represent?

IVAN: It's called: 'Mother – Fatherland!'

*They look at each other, then start laughing heartily again.
They calm down.*

It was supposed to be a portrait of my mother. It doesn't
really look like her, though, does it? Then my instructor
suggested 'Fatherland'. So to combine the two, I chose
'Mother – Fatherland'.

*RASHA, serious, takes the sculpture in his hands and looks
at it from all angles.*

RASHA: You know, this isn't all that bad!

...

Why is her mouth wide open?

IVAN: She's shouting. Warning. Scolding

...

Something's hurting her... If you like it, have it.

RASHA: I like it. I do.

IVAN: Would you like a nice cup of coffee? Or tea?

RASHA: No...! Sit yourself down, man. I'll get it.

IVAN sits down, RASHA goes into the kitchen.

IVAN: I heard your father mention the police. Are they
really coming for you?

RASHA: Coffee or tea?

IVAN: Tea!

RASHA comes back from the kitchen, sits down.

RASHA: If they do come, you'll protect me… Won't you?

IVAN is serious. Dark and determined.

IVAN: I will.

RASHA: I love your poem. It's excellent.

IVAN: 'The Snail'?

RASHA: 'The Snail'.

IVAN: The sculpture, too?

RASHA: 'Mother – Fatherland'?

IVAN: 'Mother – Fatherland'…

They look at each other. Then they laugh for a long time, until they cry.

The End.